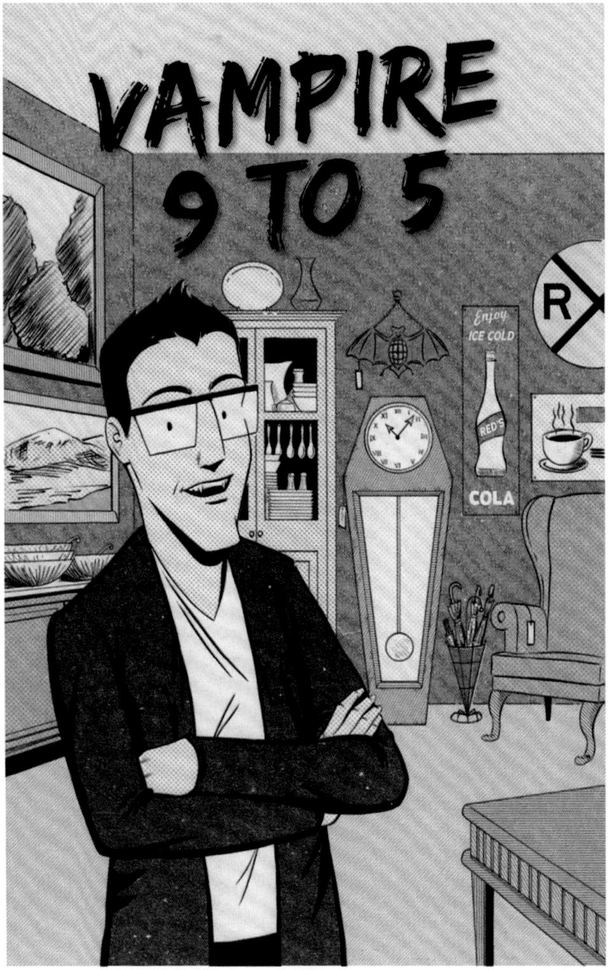
VAMPIRE
9 TO 5
R
Enjoy
ICE COLD
RED'S
COLA

By Ben Nussbaum
Illustrated by Joseph McDermott

Publishing Credits

Rachelle Cracchiolo, M.S.Ed., *Publisher*
Conni Medina, M.A.Ed., *Editor in Chief*
Nika Fabienke, Ed.D., *Content Director*
Véronique Bos, *Creative Director*
Shaun N. Bernadou, *Art Director*
Noelle Cristea, M.A.Ed., *Senior Editor*
John Leach, *Assistant Editor*
Jess Johnson, *Graphic Designer*

Image Credits

Illustrated by Joseph McDermott

Library of Congress Cataloging-in-Publication Data

Names: Nussbaum, Ben, 1975- author. | McDermott, Joseph, illustrator.
Title: Vampire 9 to 5 / by Ben Nussbaum ; illustrated by Joseph McDermott.
Other titles: Vampire nine to five
Description: Huntington Beach, CA : Teacher Created Materials, [2020] |
  Includes book club questions. | Audience: Age 9. | Audience: Grades 4-6.
Identifiers: LCCN 2019035578 (print) | LCCN 2019035579 (ebook) | ISBN
  9781644913666 (paperback) | ISBN 9781644914564 (ebook)
Subjects: LCSH: Readers (Elementary) | Vampires--Juvenile fiction.
Classification: LCC PE1119 .N878 2020 (print) | LCC PE1119 (ebook) | DDC
  428.6/2--dc23
LC record available at https://lccn.loc.gov/2019035578
LC ebook record available at https://lccn.loc.gov/2019035579

Note: All companies, websites, and products mentioned in this book are registered trademarks of their respective owners or developers and are used in this book strictly for editorial purposes. No commercial claim to their use is made by the author or the publisher.

TCM Teacher Created Materials

5301 Oceanus Drive
Huntington Beach, CA 92649-1030
www.tcmpub.com

ISBN 978-1-6449-1366-6
© 2020 Teacher Created Materials, Inc.

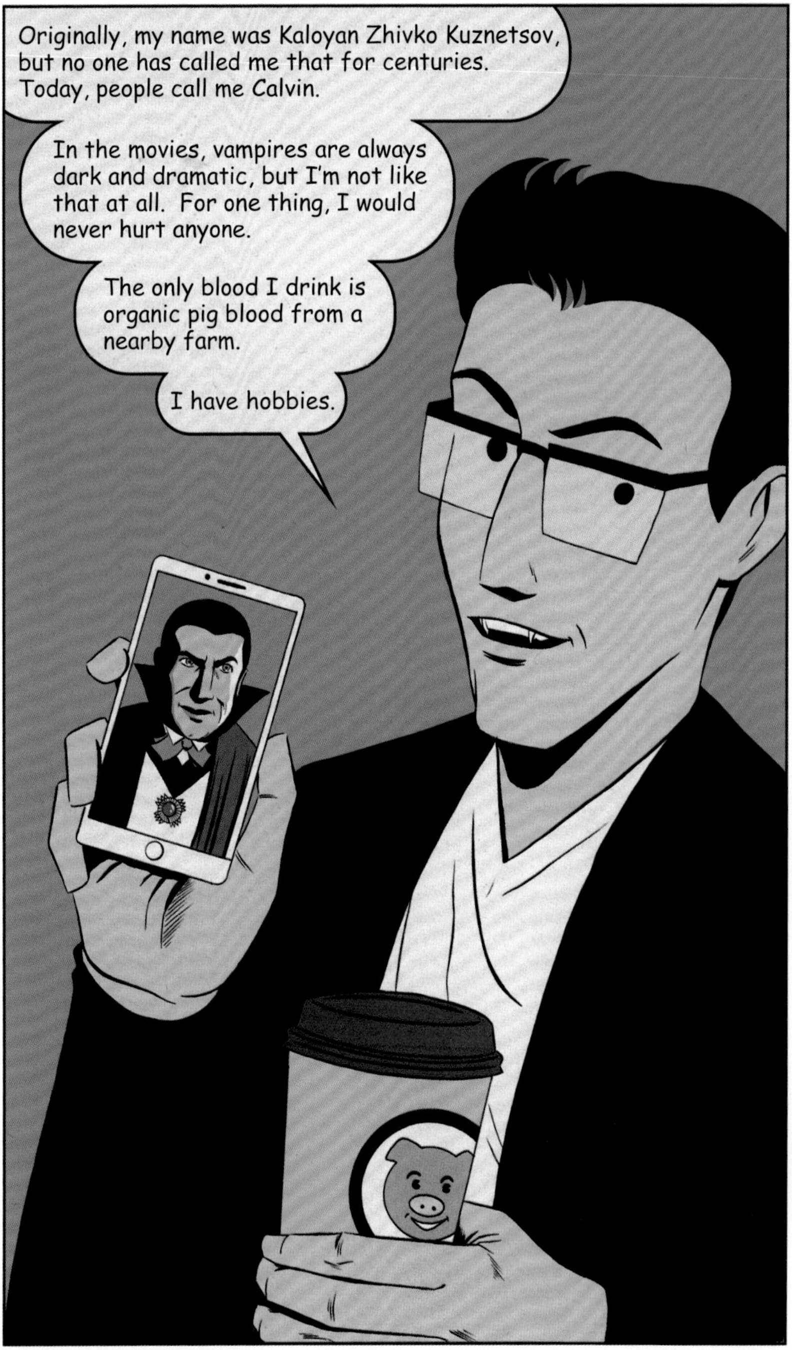
Originally, my name was Kaloyan Zhivko Kuznetsov, but no one has called me that for centuries. Today, people call me Calvin.
In the movies, vampires are always dark and dramatic, but I'm not like that at all. For one thing, I would never hurt anyone.
The only blood I drink is organic pig blood from a nearby farm.
I have hobbies.

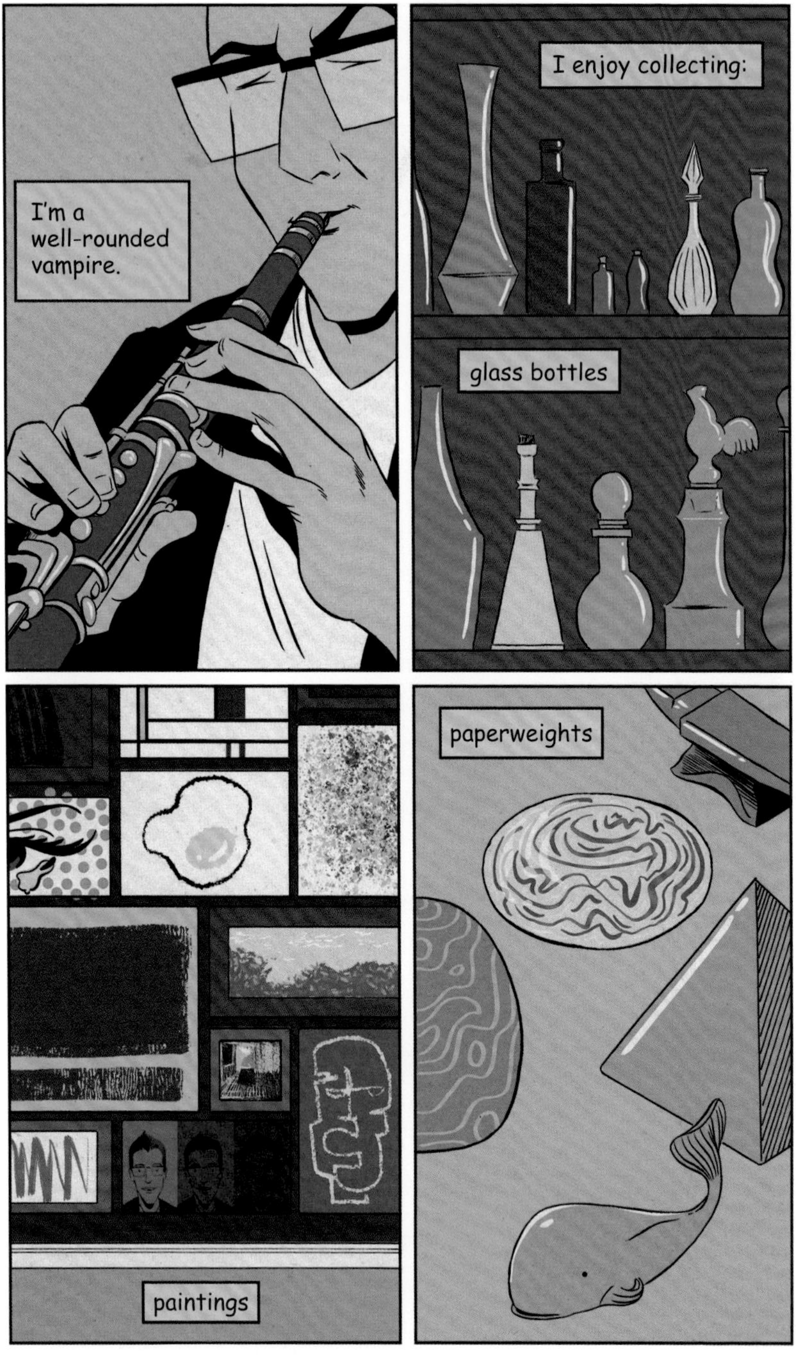
I'm a well-rounded vampire.
I enjoy collecting:
glass bottles
paintings
paperweights

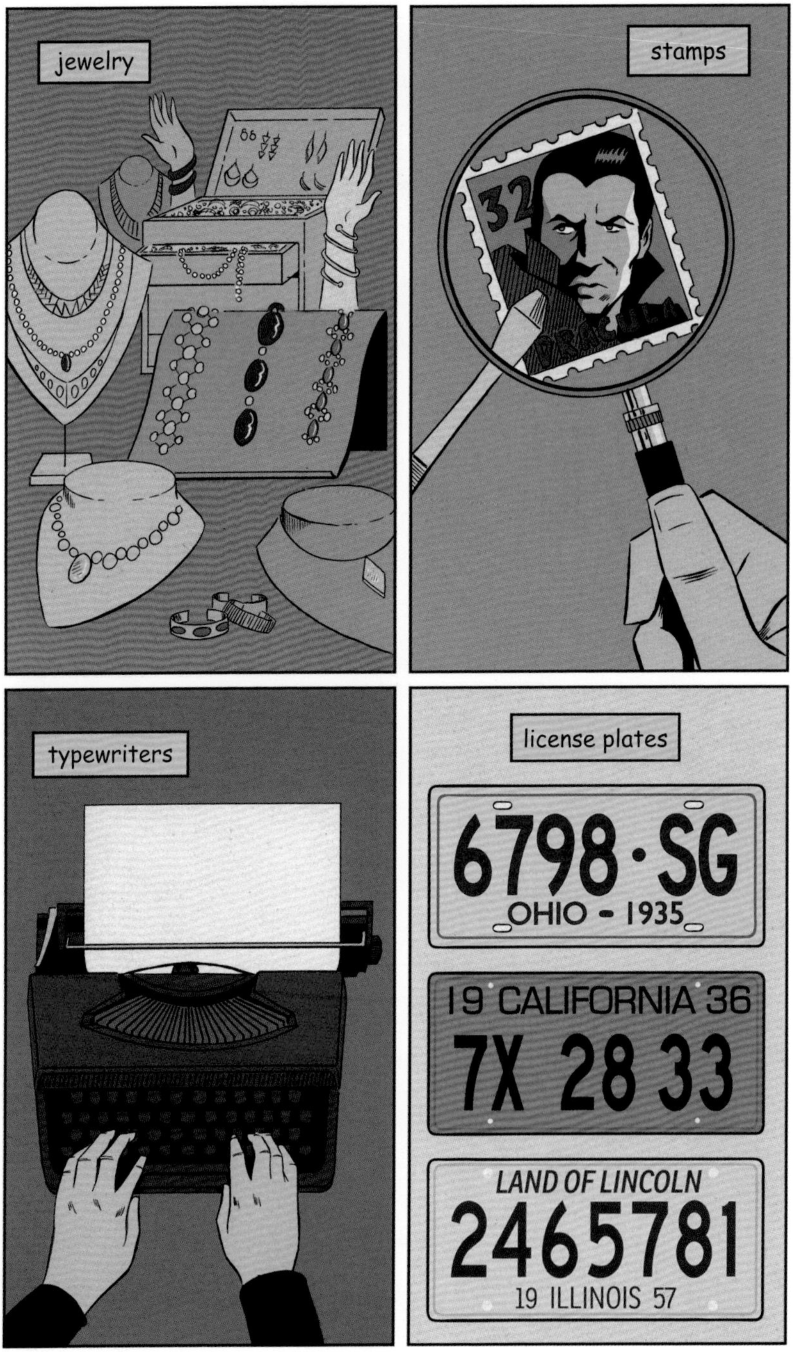
jewelry
stamps
32
DRACULA
typewriters
license plates
6798 · SG
OHIO - 1935
19 CALIFORNIA 36
7X 28 33
LAND OF LINCOLN
2465781
19 ILLINOIS 57

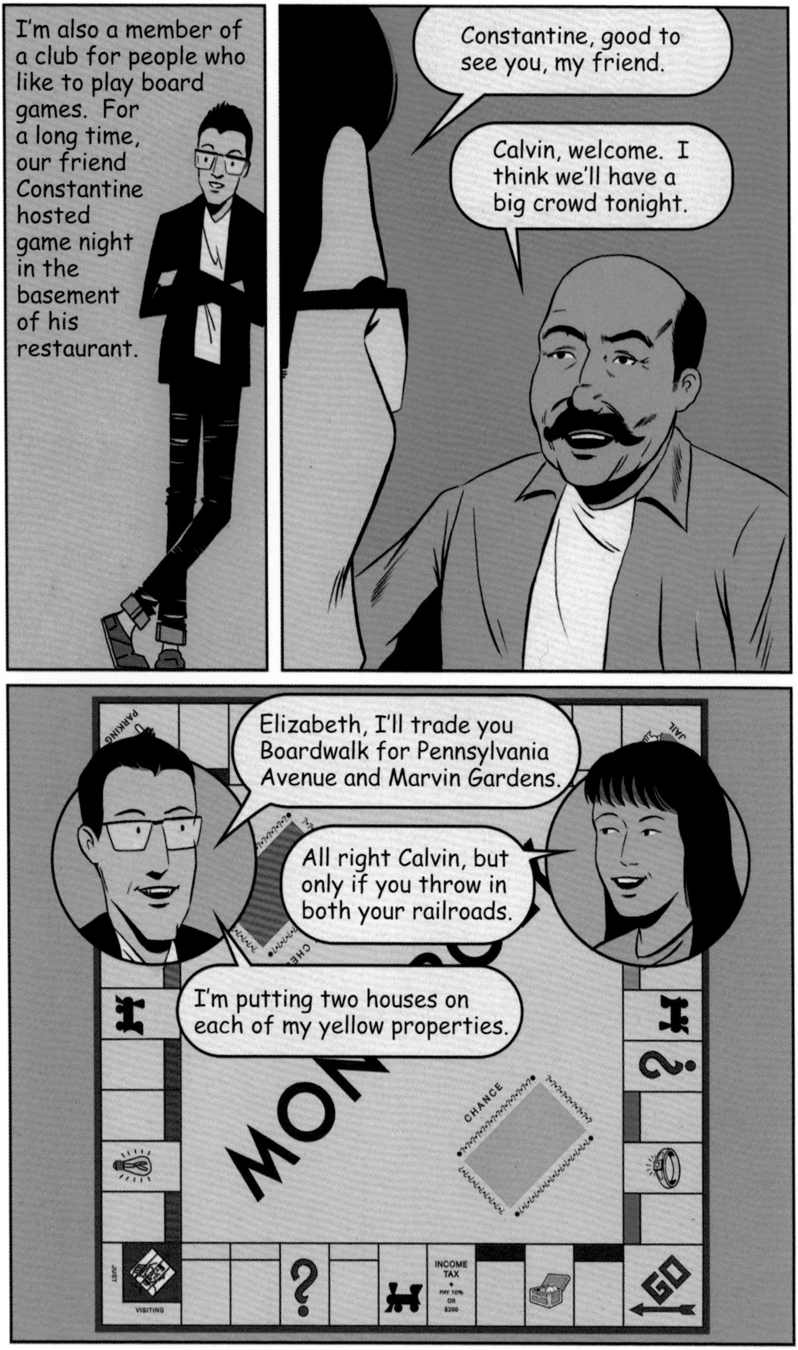
I'm also a member of a club for people who like to play board games. For a long time, our friend Constantine hosted game night in the basement of his restaurant.
Constantine, good to see you, my friend.
Calvin, welcome. I think we'll have a big crowd tonight.
Elizabeth, I'll trade you Boardwalk for Pennsylvania Avenue and Marvin Gardens.
All right Calvin, but only if you throw in both your railroads.
I'm putting two houses on each of my yellow properties.
PARKING
JAIL
CHANCE
JUST
VISITING
INCOME TAX
GO

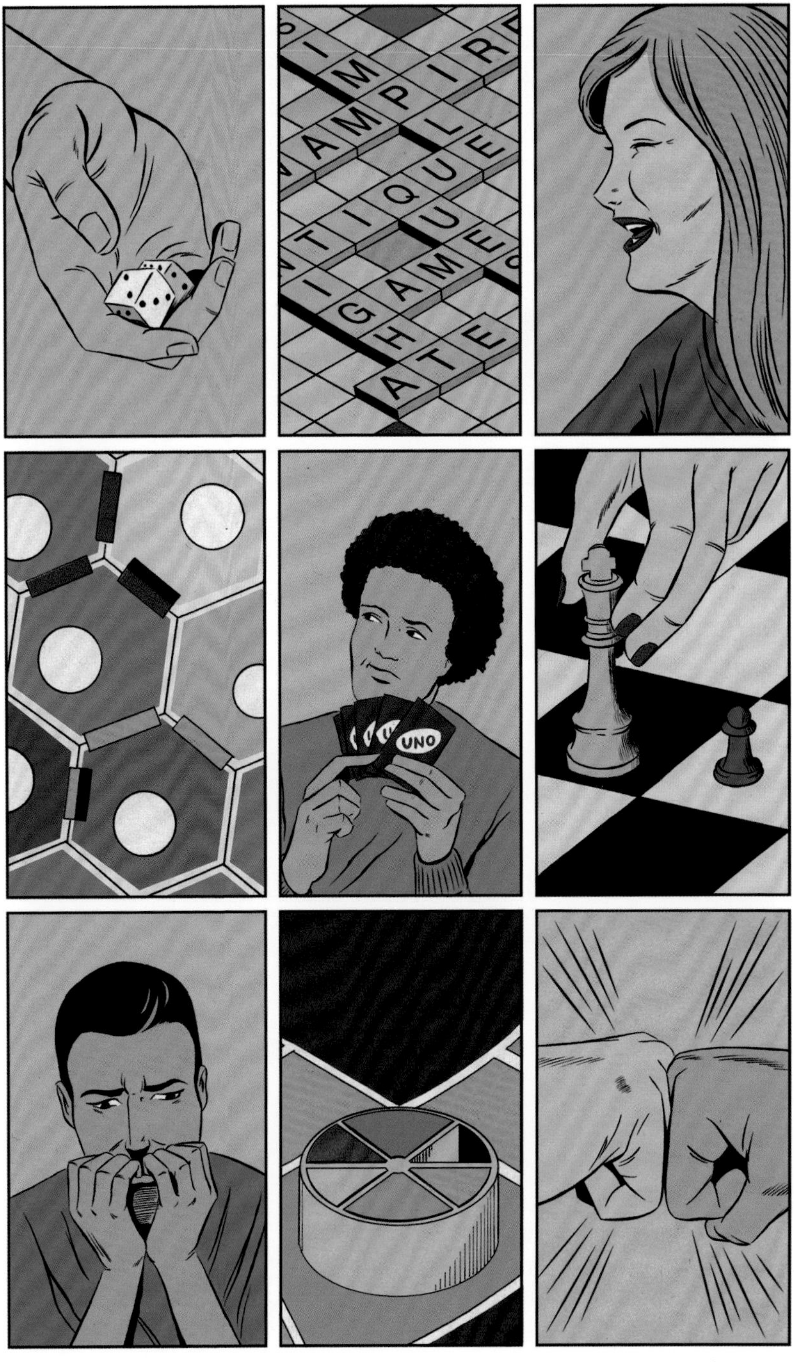
GAME
UNO

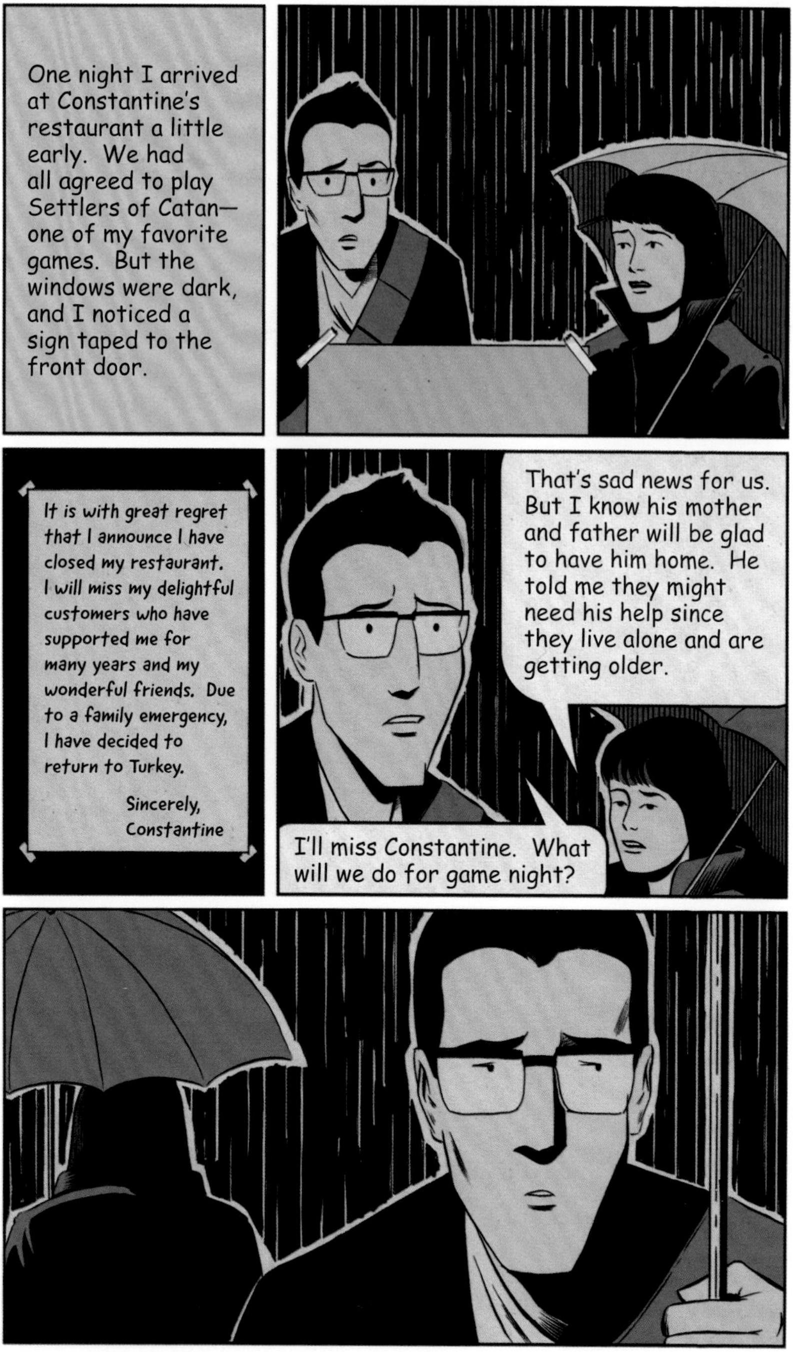
One night I arrived at Constantine's restaurant a little early. We had all agreed to play Settlers of Catan—one of my favorite games. But the windows were dark, and I noticed a sign taped to the front door.
It is with great regret that I announce I have closed my restaurant. I will miss my delightful customers who have supported me for many years and my wonderful friends. Due to a family emergency, I have decided to return to Turkey.
Sincerely, Constantine
I'll miss Constantine. What will we do for game night?
That's sad news for us. But I know his mother and father will be glad to have him home. He told me they might need his help since they live alone and are getting older.

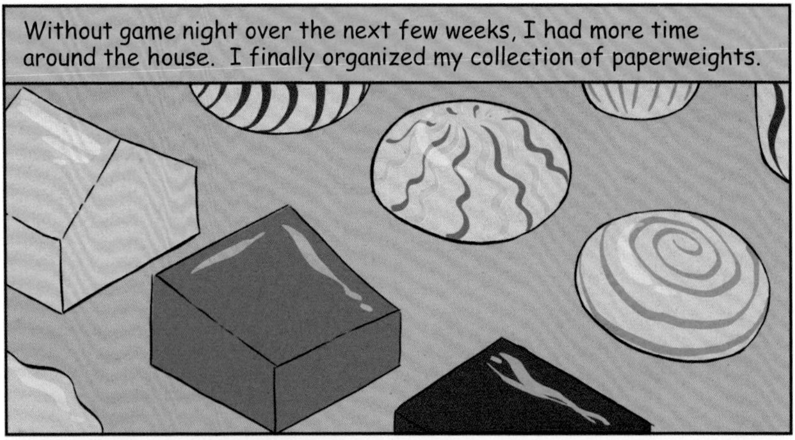
Without game night over the next few weeks, I had more time around the house. I finally organized my collection of paperweights.

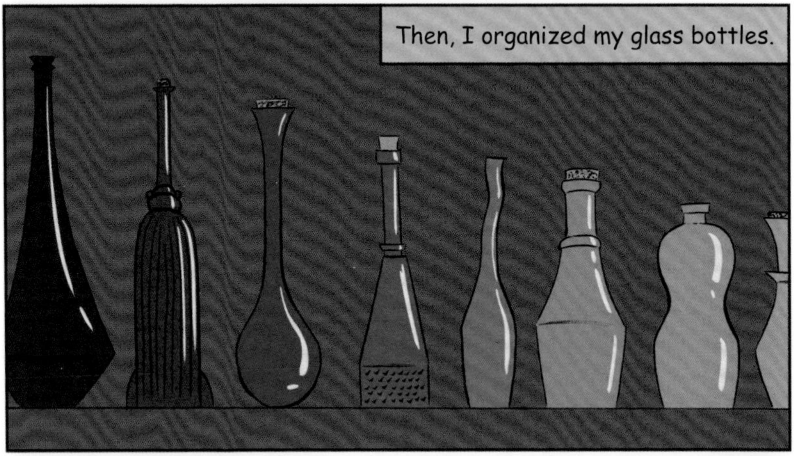
Then, I organized my glass bottles.

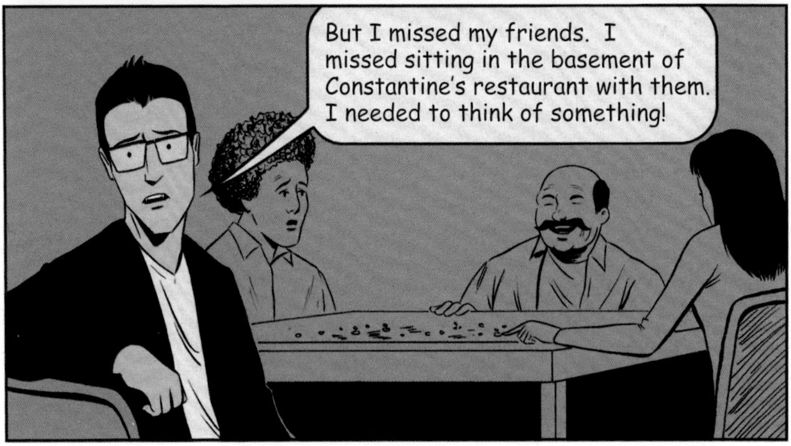
But I missed my friends. I missed sitting in the basement of Constantine's restaurant with them. I needed to think of something!

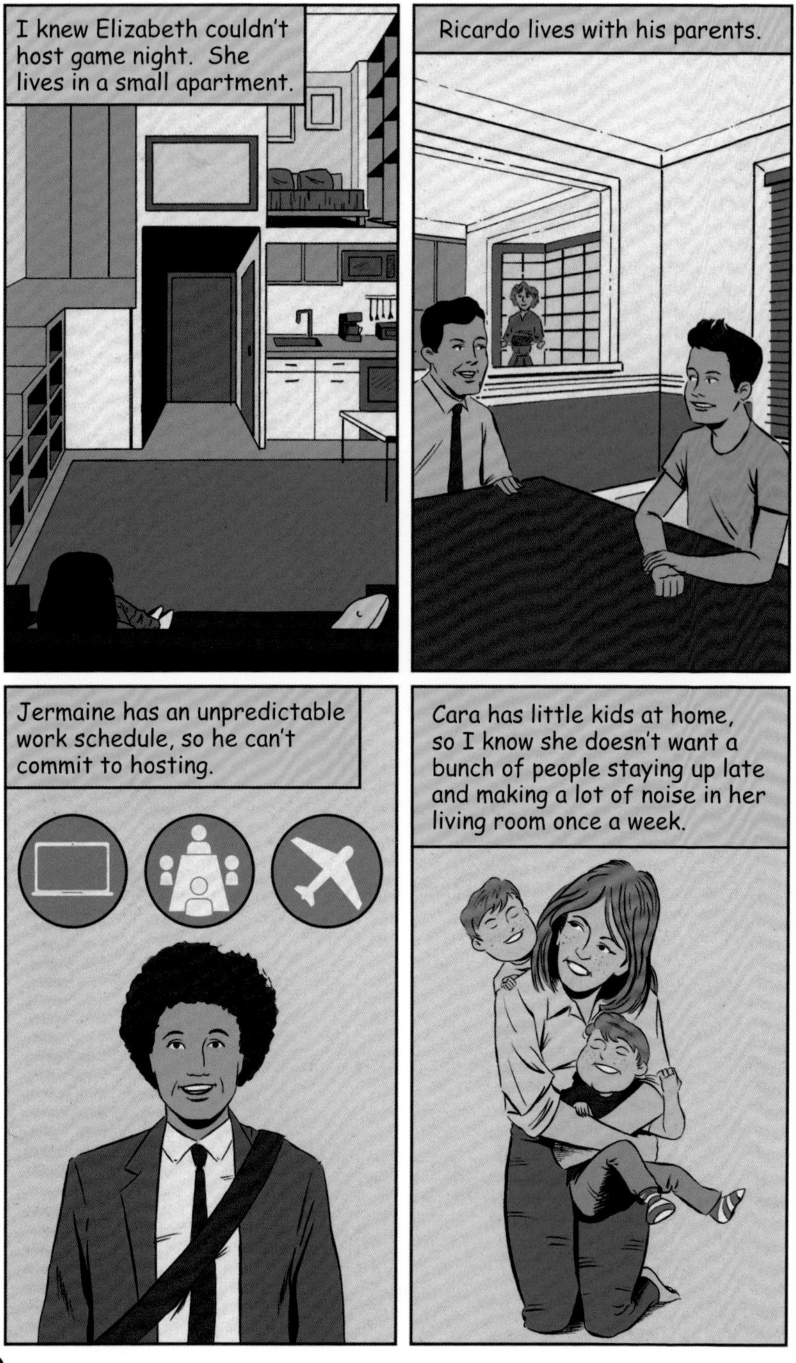
I knew Elizabeth couldn't host game night. She lives in a small apartment.
Ricardo lives with his parents.
Jermaine has an unpredictable work schedule, so he can't commit to hosting.
Cara has little kids at home, so I know she doesn't want a bunch of people staying up late and making a lot of noise in her living room once a week.

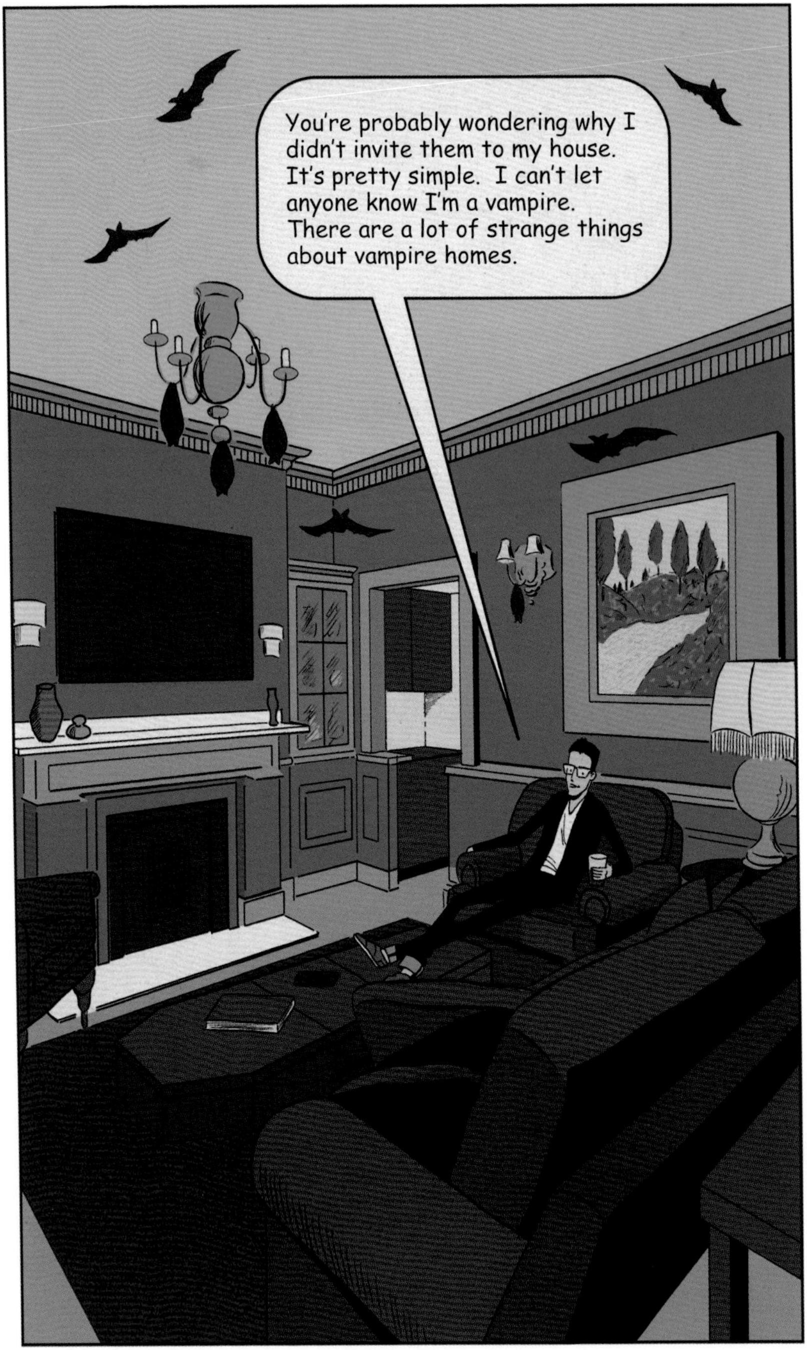
You're probably wondering why I didn't invite them to my house. It's pretty simple. I can't let anyone know I'm a vampire. There are a lot of strange things about vampire homes.

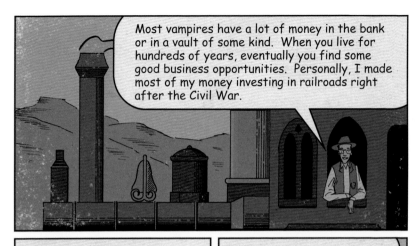

Most vampires have a lot of money in the bank or in a vault of some kind. When you live for hundreds of years, eventually you find some good business opportunities. Personally, I made most of my money investing in railroads right after the Civil War.

So I had a little money saved up. It was nothing too impressive, but enough that I started thinking about opening up some kind of business of my own. Like Constantine's restaurant, it would be a place where we could all play together.

Opening a restaurant of my own didn't make a lot of sense. Vampires can't eat food.

Calvin, please, just once?

You must try the food. You own the restaurant!

I thought about opening a yoga studio.

But there are so many studios...

DRACULA

THE VAMPYRE

INTERVIEW WITH THE VAMPIRE

VAMPIRE CITY

The idea of opening a bookstore was intriguing too. I do read quite a lot. And have you ever noticed how wonderful bookstores smell?

12

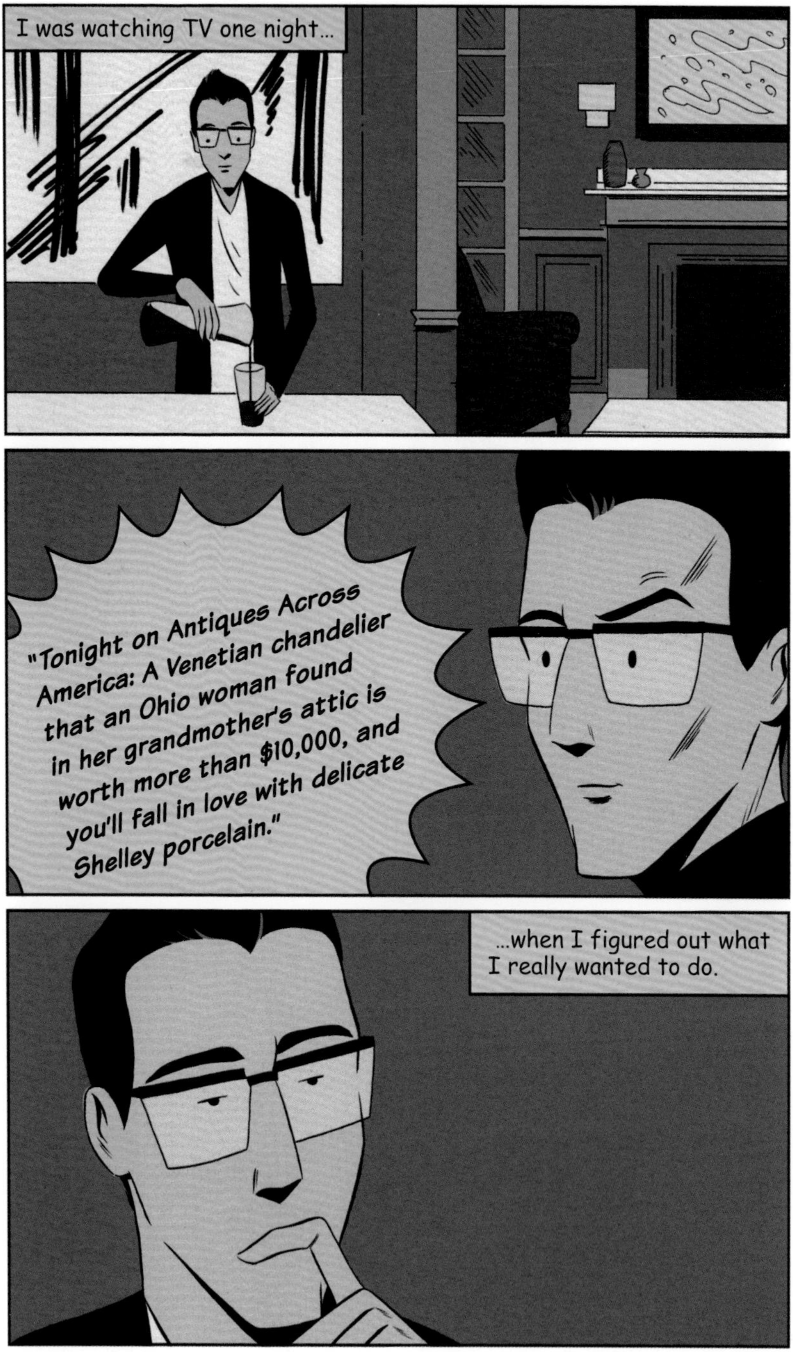
I was watching TV one night...
"Tonight on Antiques Across America: A Venetian chandelier that an Ohio woman found in her grandmother's attic is worth more than $10,000, and you'll fall in love with delicate Shelley porcelain."
...when I figured out what I really wanted to do.

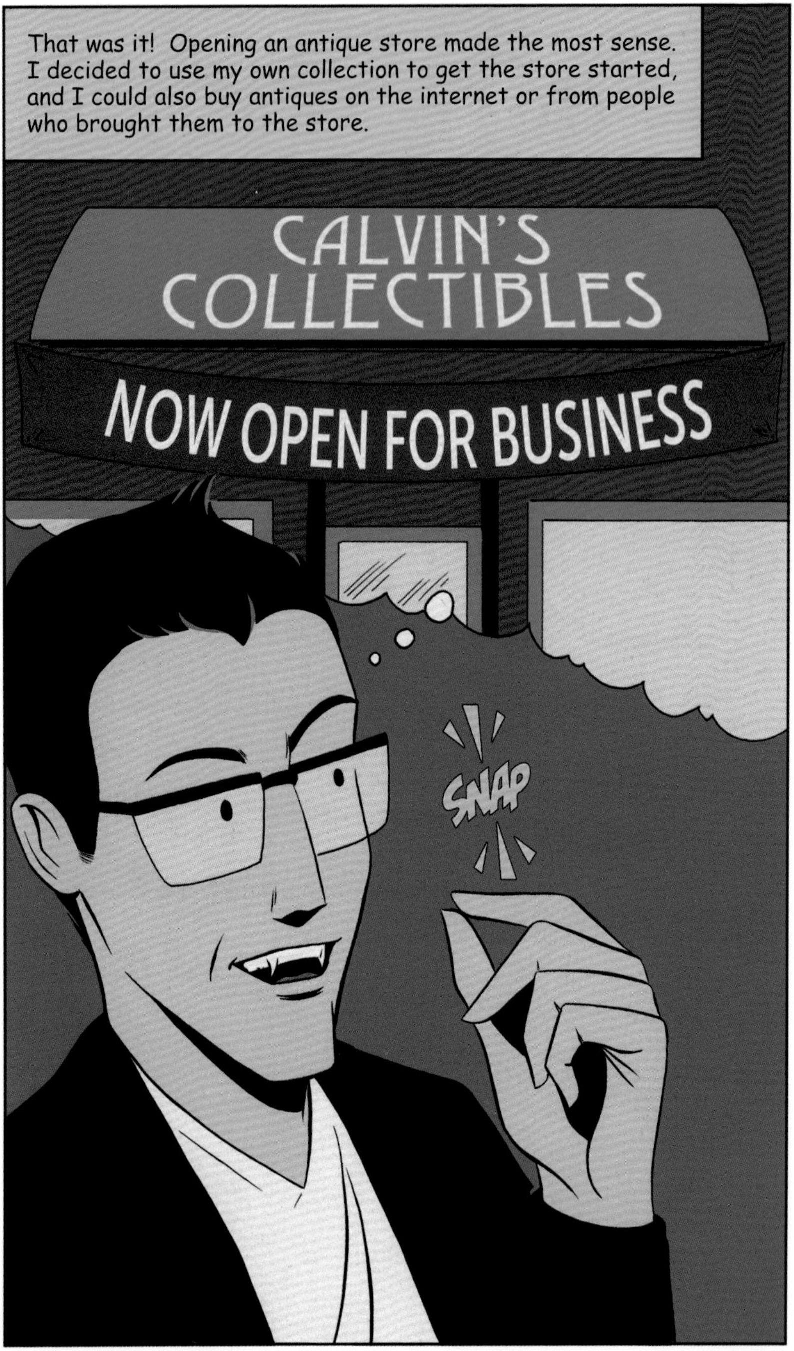
That was it! Opening an antique store made the most sense. I decided to use my own collection to get the store started, and I could also buy antiques on the internet or from people who brought them to the store.
CALVIN'S COLLECTIBLES
NOW OPEN FOR BUSINESS
SNAP

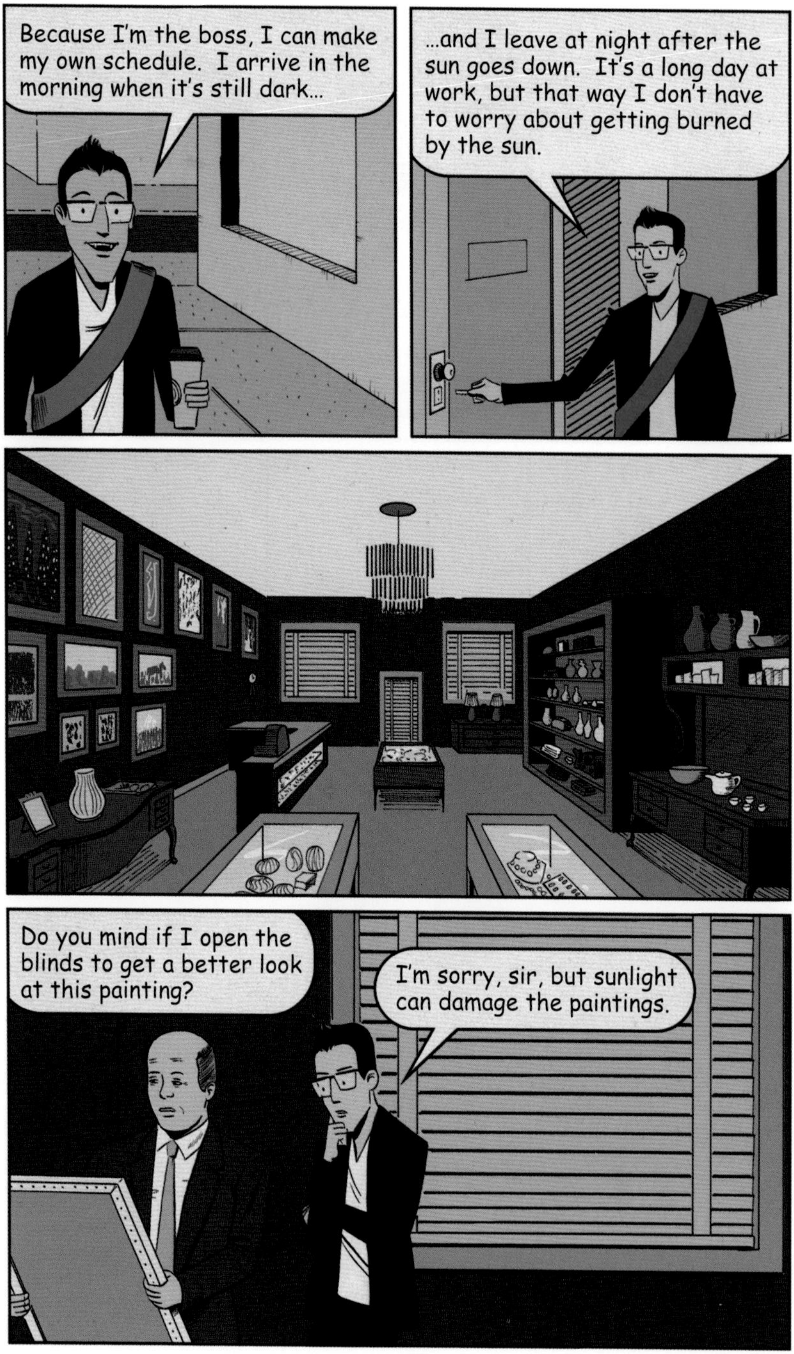
Because I'm the boss, I can make my own schedule. I arrive in the morning when it's still dark...
...and I leave at night after the sun goes down. It's a long day at work, but that way I don't have to worry about getting burned by the sun.
Do you mind if I open the blinds to get a better look at this painting?
I'm sorry, sir, but sunlight can damage the paintings.

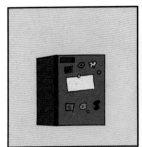

I've got the store set up so that it's very comfortable for me. A little refrigerator for organic pig blood, an office without any windows, and some nice speakers so I can listen to music while I work. I even have a comfortable chair.

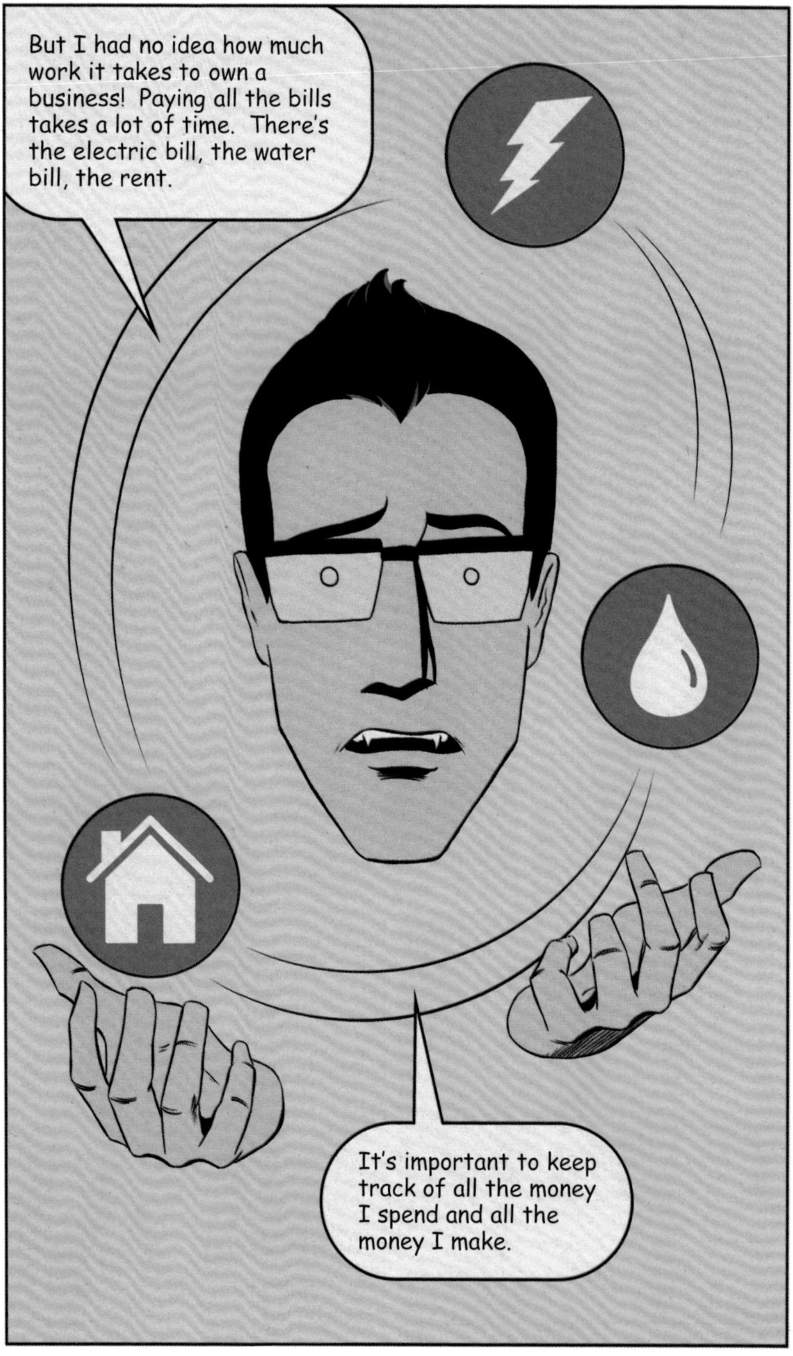
But I had no idea how much work it takes to own a business! Paying all the bills takes a lot of time. There's the electric bill, the water bill, the rent.
It's important to keep track of all the money I spend and all the money I make.

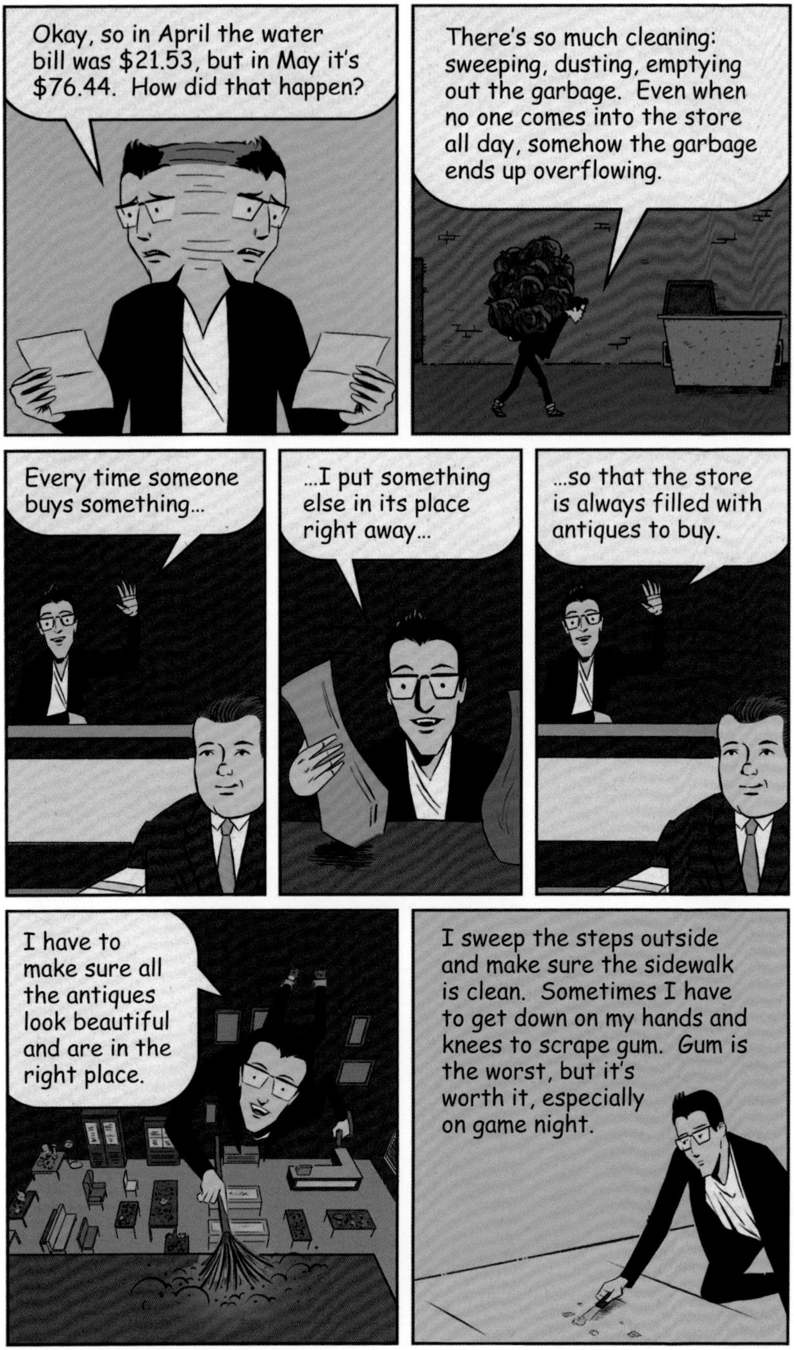
Okay, so in April the water bill was $21.53, but in May it's $76.44. How did that happen?
There's so much cleaning: sweeping, dusting, emptying out the garbage. Even when no one comes into the store all day, somehow the garbage ends up overflowing.
Every time someone buys something...
...I put something else in its place right away...
...so that the store is always filled with antiques to buy.
I have to make sure all the antiques look beautiful and are in the right place.
I sweep the steps outside and make sure the sidewalk is clean. Sometimes I have to get down on my hands and knees to scrape gum. Gum is the worst, but it's worth it, especially on game night.

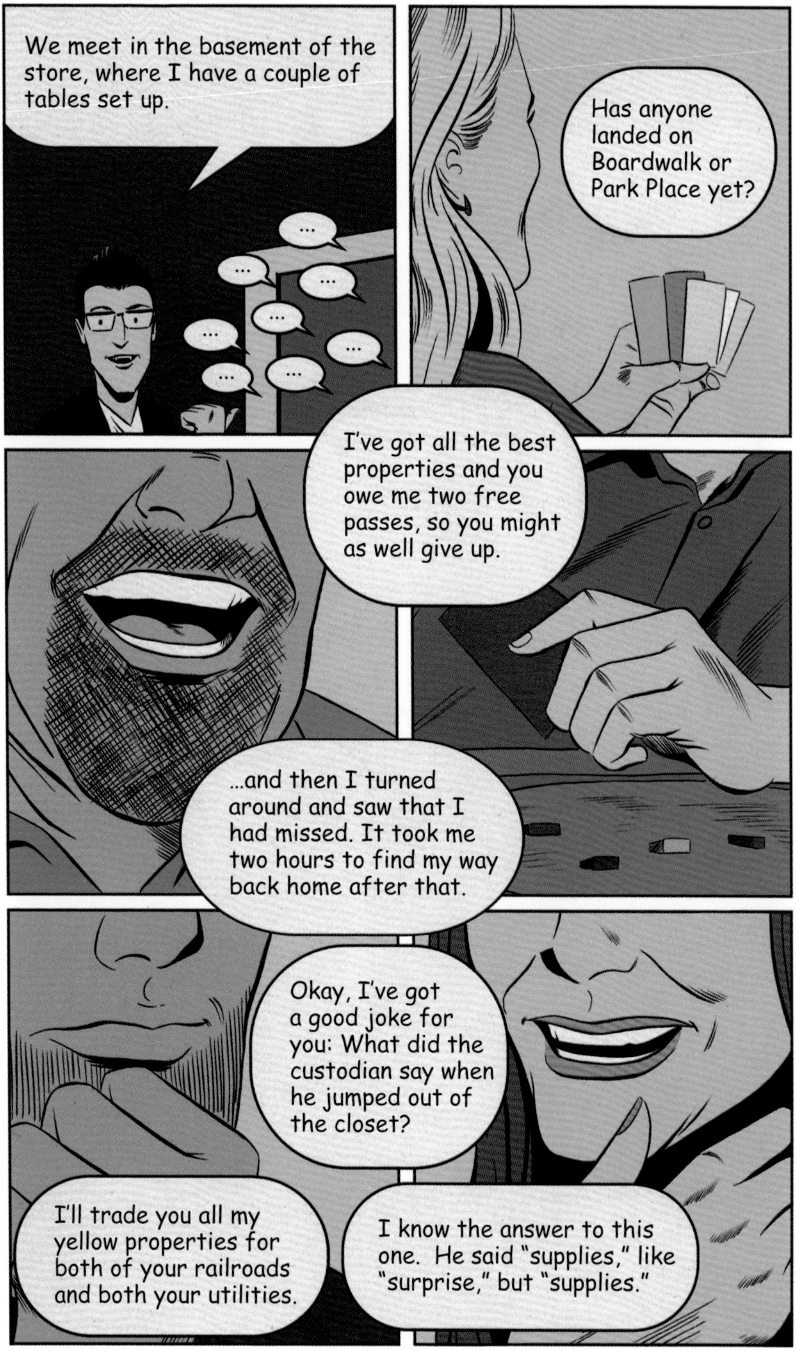
We meet in the basement of the store, where I have a couple of tables set up.
...
...
...
...
...
...
...
...
Has anyone landed on Boardwalk or Park Place yet?
I've got all the best properties and you owe me two free passes, so you might as well give up.
...and then I turned around and saw that I had missed. It took me two hours to find my way back home after that.
Okay, I've got a good joke for you: What did the custodian say when he jumped out of the closet?
I'll trade you all my yellow properties for both of your railroads and both your utilities.
I know the answer to this one. He said "supplies," like "surprise," but "supplies."

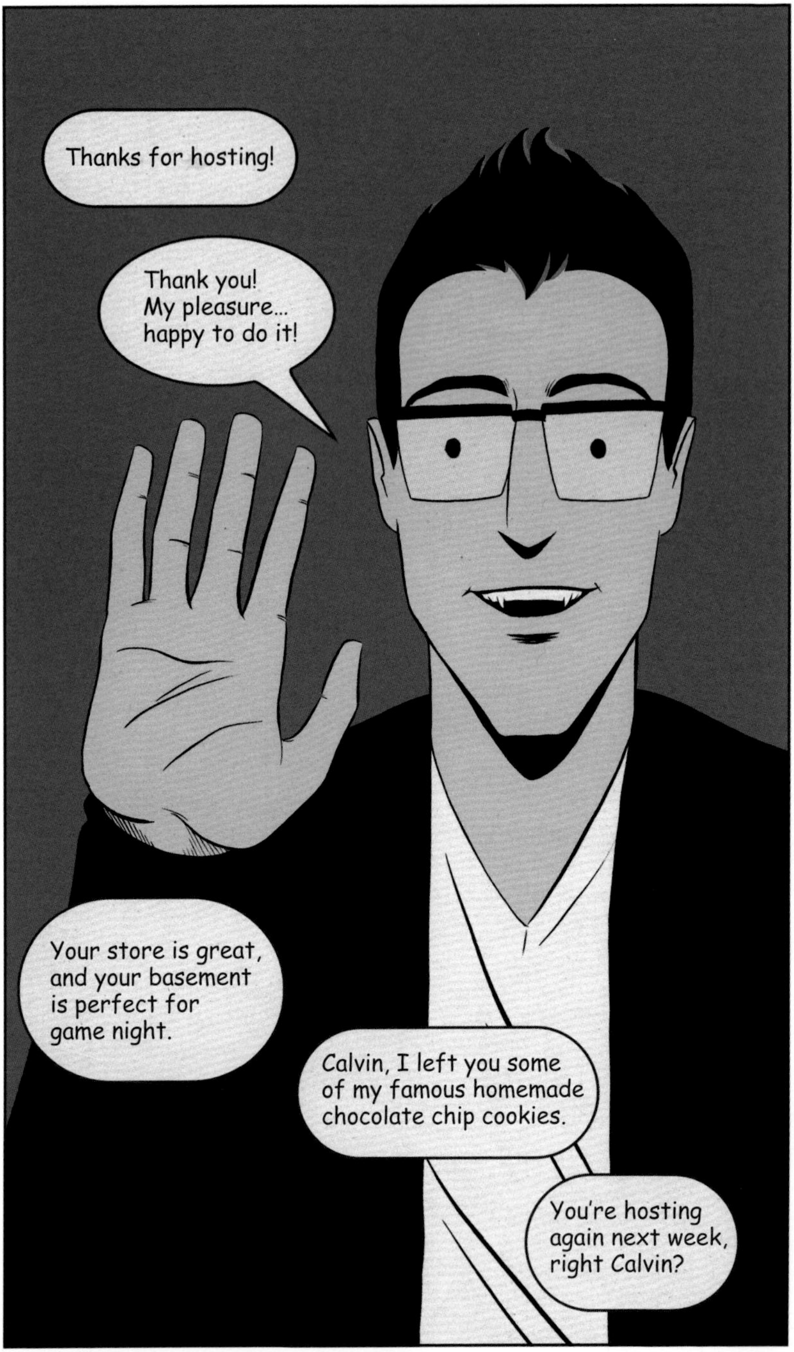
Thanks for hosting!
Thank you! My pleasure... happy to do it!
Your store is great, and your basement is perfect for game night.
Calvin, I left you some of my famous homemade chocolate chip cookies.
You're hosting again next week, right Calvin?

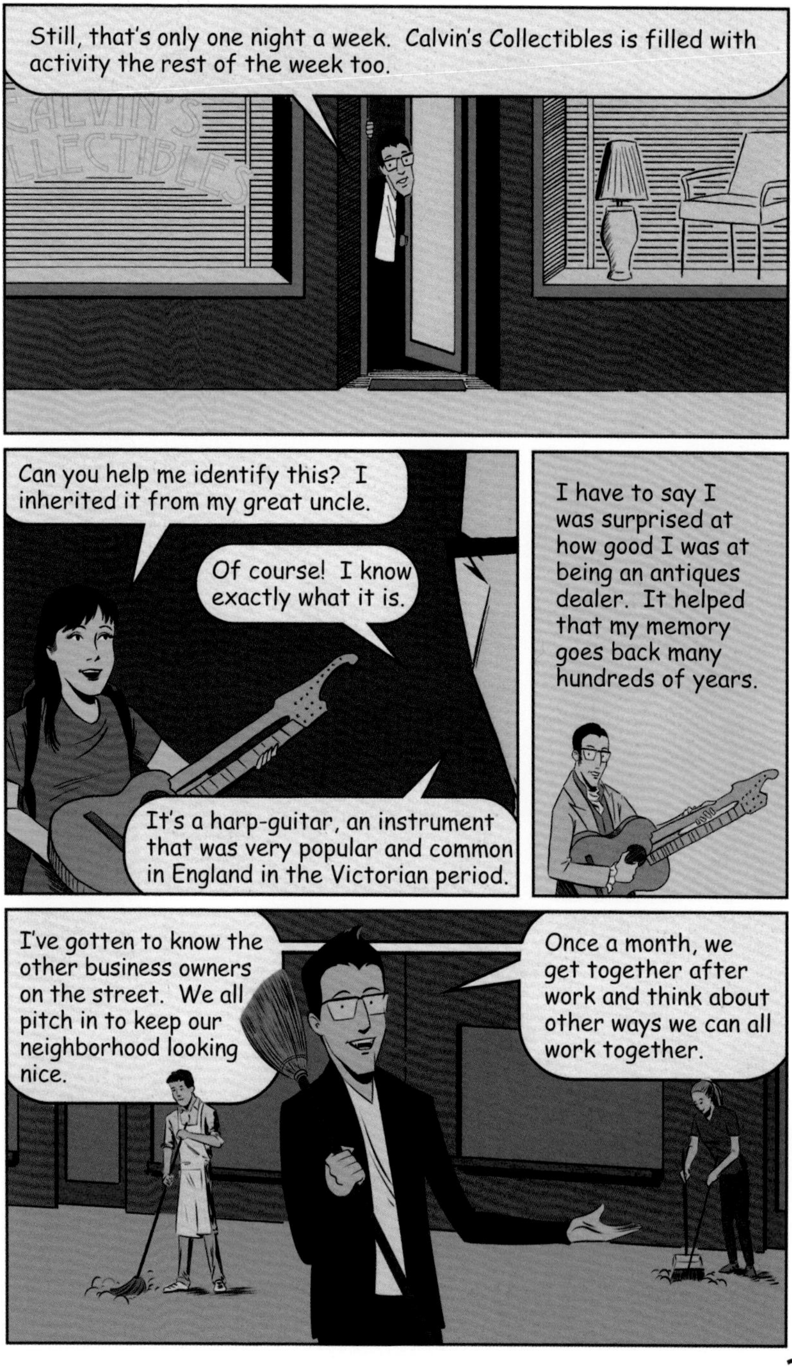
Still, that's only one night a week. Calvin's Collectibles is filled with activity the rest of the week too.
CALVIN'S COLLECTIBLES
Can you help me identify this? I inherited it from my great uncle.
Of course! I know exactly what it is.
It's a harp-guitar, an instrument that was very popular and common in England in the Victorian period.
I have to say I was surprised at how good I was at being an antiques dealer. It helped that my memory goes back many hundreds of years.
I've gotten to know the other business owners on the street. We all pitch in to keep our neighborhood looking nice.
Once a month, we get together after work and think about other ways we can all work together.

I had a lot on my plate. I liked being busy, but I was a little too busy. I decided I needed some help around the store.

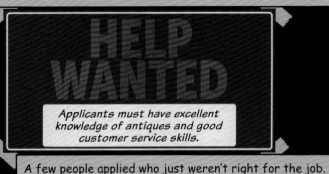

Applicants must have excellent knowledge of antiques and good customer service skills.

A few people applied who just weren't right for the job.

I didn't know I'd have to work weekends!

So, like, what happens if I break something?

Could I work part-time, or do you offer daycare?

And then, Beverly applied. She's very chatty and fun to talk with, she works hard, she's reliable, and she knows a lot about antiques.

Good morning Calvin, how are you? I had the most wonderful walk here this morning with the sun out and the birds chirping and...

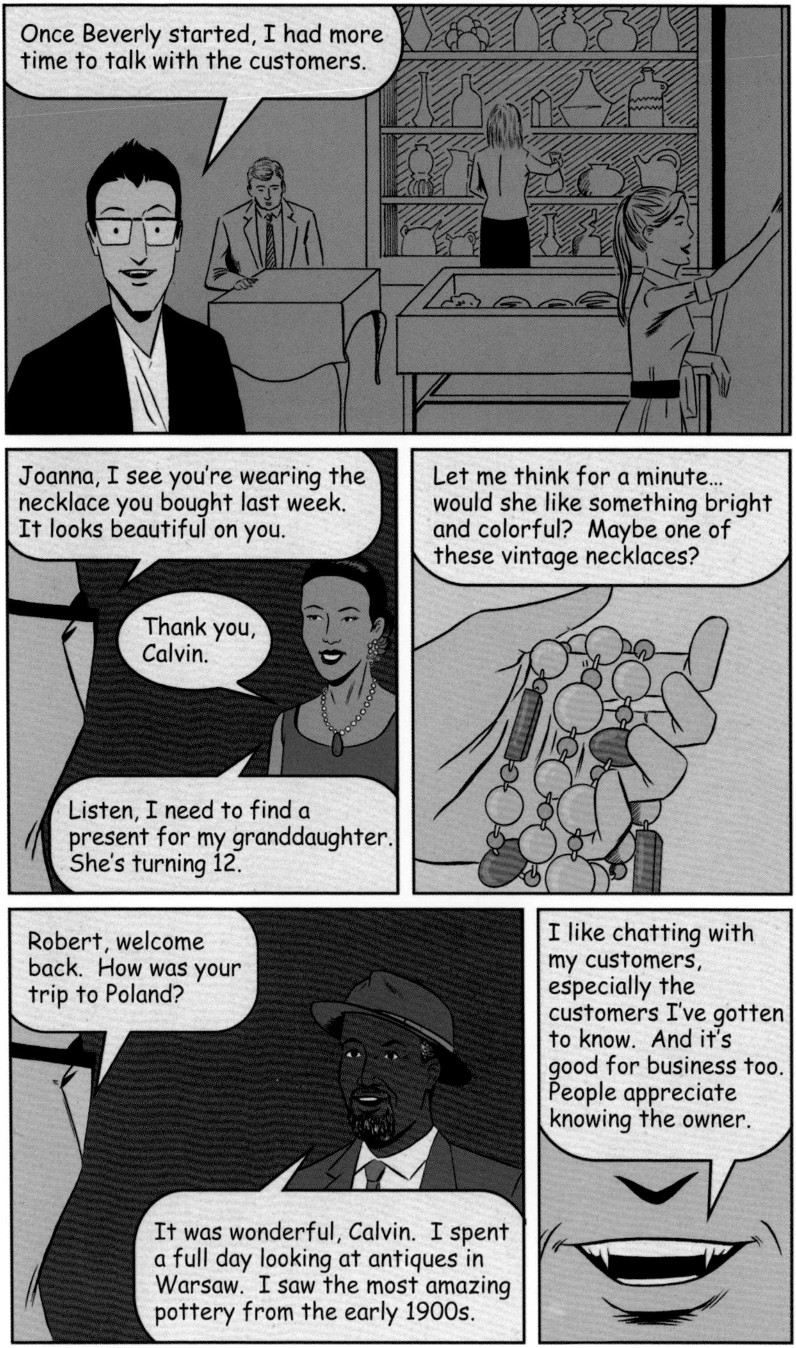
Once Beverly started, I had more time to talk with the customers.
Joanna, I see you're wearing the necklace you bought last week. It looks beautiful on you.
Thank you, Calvin.
Listen, I need to find a present for my granddaughter. She's turning 12.
Let me think for a minute... would she like something bright and colorful? Maybe one of these vintage necklaces?
Robert, welcome back. How was your trip to Poland?
It was wonderful, Calvin. I spent a full day looking at antiques in Warsaw. I saw the most amazing pottery from the early 1900s.
I like chatting with my customers, especially the customers I've gotten to know. And it's good for business too. People appreciate knowing the owner.

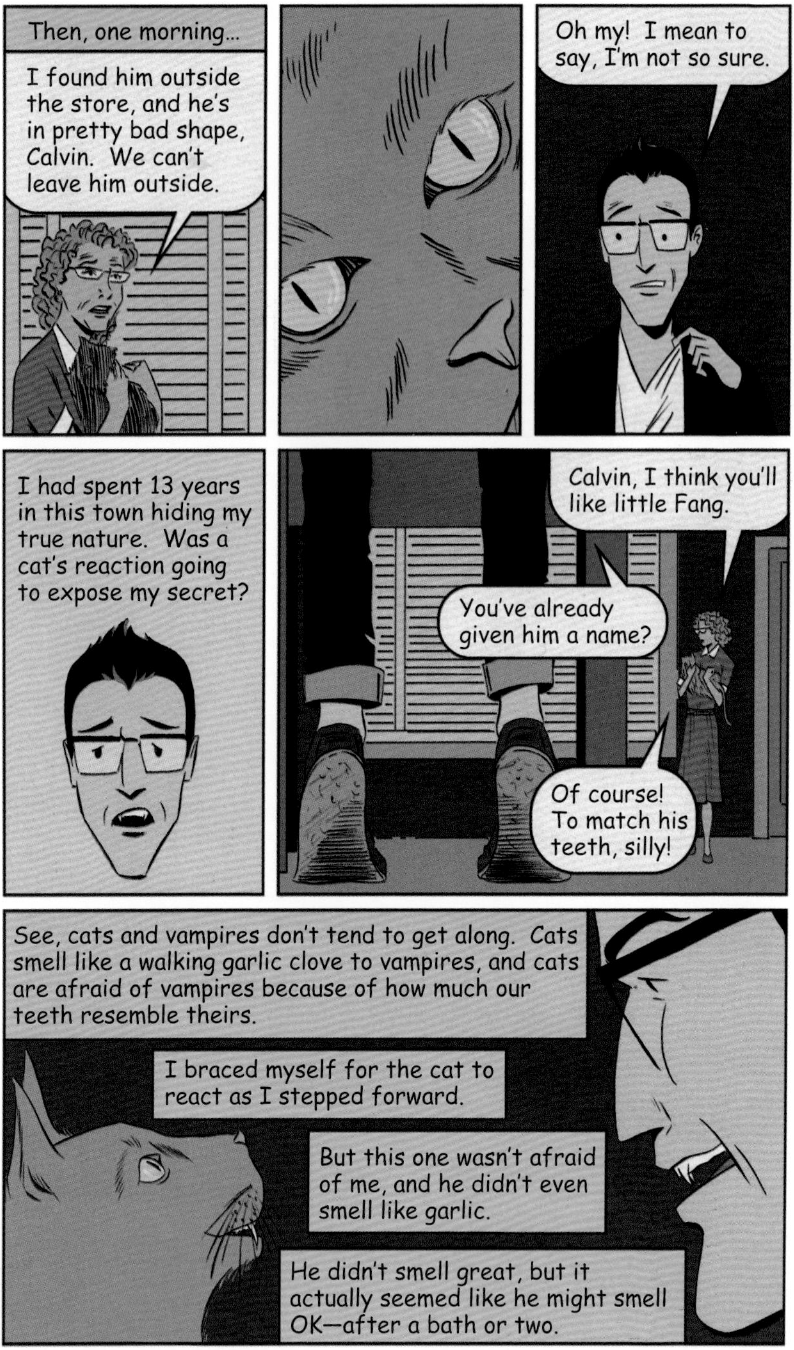

Then, one morning...
I found him outside the store, and he's in pretty bad shape, Calvin. We can't leave him outside.
Oh my! I mean to say, I'm not so sure.
I had spent 13 years in this town hiding my true nature. Was a cat's reaction going to expose my secret?
Calvin, I think you'll like little Fang.
You've already given him a name?
Of course! To match his teeth, silly!
See, cats and vampires don't tend to get along. Cats smell like a walking garlic clove to vampires, and cats are afraid of vampires because of how much our teeth resemble theirs.
I braced myself for the cat to react as I stepped forward.
But this one wasn't afraid of me, and he didn't even smell like garlic.
He didn't smell great, but it actually seemed like he might smell OK—after a bath or two.

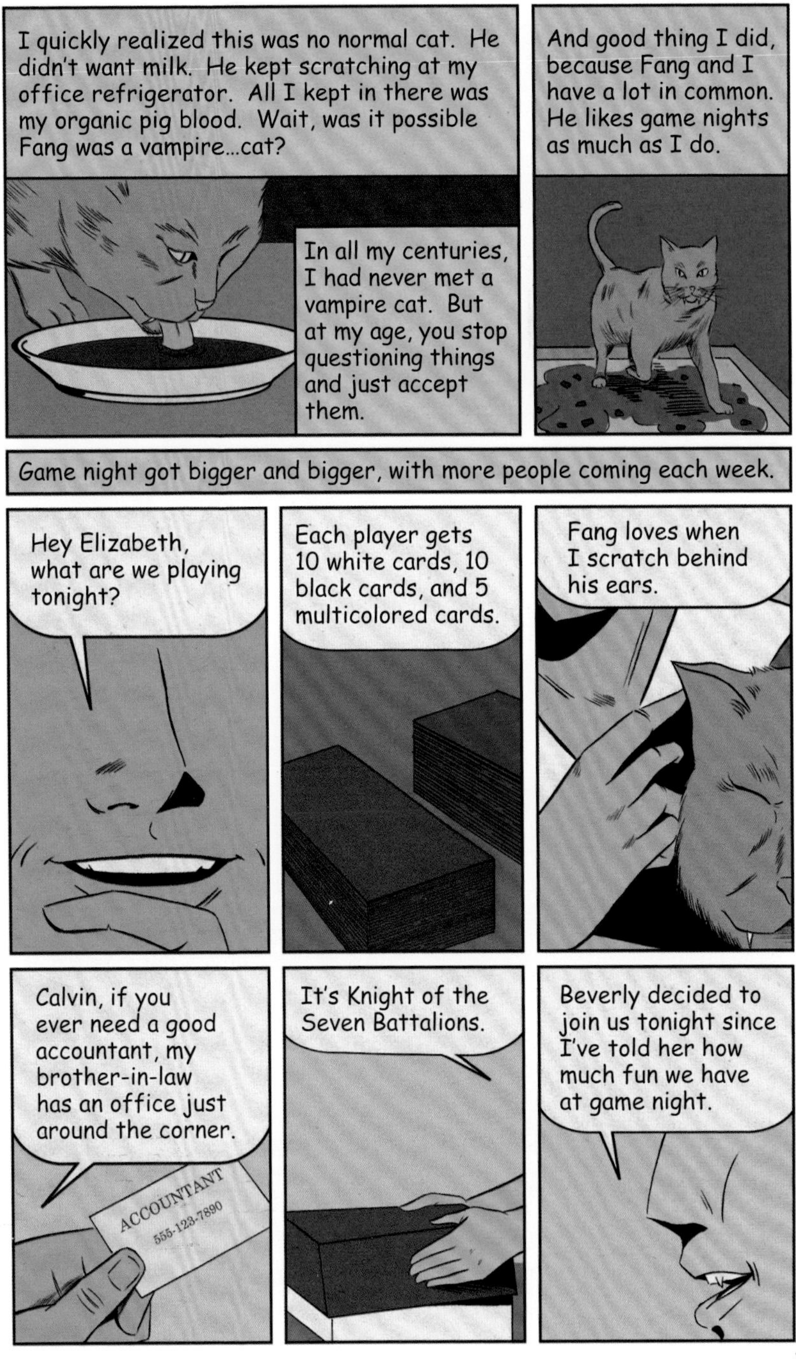
I quickly realized this was no normal cat. He didn't want milk. He kept scratching at my office refrigerator. All I kept in there was my organic pig blood. Wait, was it possible Fang was a vampire...cat?
In all my centuries, I had never met a vampire cat. But at my age, you stop questioning things and just accept them.
And good thing I did, because Fang and I have a lot in common. He likes game nights as much as I do.
Game night got bigger and bigger, with more people coming each week.
Hey Elizabeth, what are we playing tonight?
Each player gets 10 white cards, 10 black cards, and 5 multicolored cards.
Fang loves when I scratch behind his ears.
Calvin, if you ever need a good accountant, my brother-in-law has an office just around the corner.
ACCOUNTANT
555-123-7890
It's Knight of the Seven Battalions.
Beverly decided to join us tonight since I've told her how much fun we have at game night.

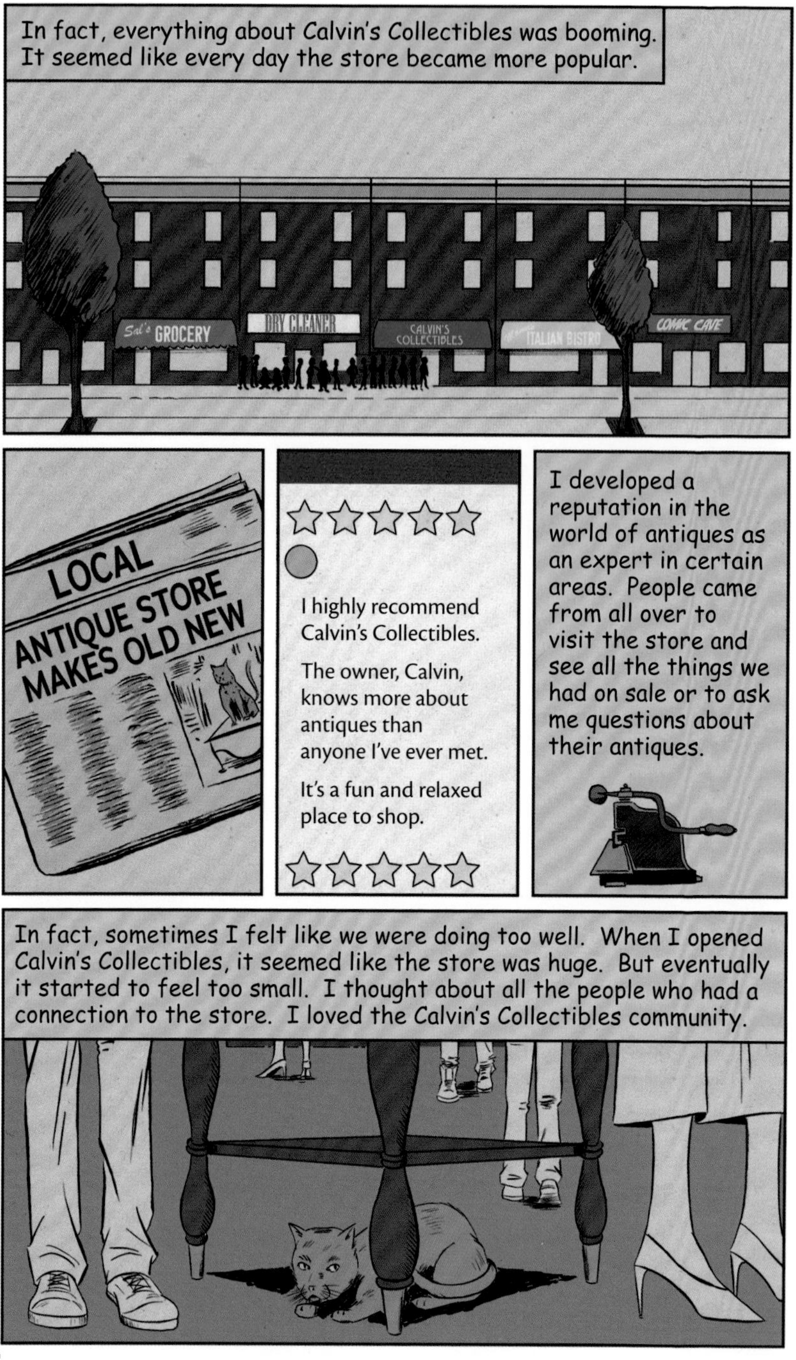
In fact, everything about Calvin's Collectibles was booming. It seemed like every day the store became more popular.
Sal's GROCERY
DRY CLEANER
CALVIN'S COLLECTIBLES
ITALIAN BISTRO
COMIC CAVE
LOCAL
ANTIQUE STORE MAKES OLD NEW
I highly recommend Calvin's Collectibles.
The owner, Calvin, knows more about antiques than anyone I've ever met.
It's a fun and relaxed place to shop.
I developed a reputation in the world of antiques as an expert in certain areas. People came from all over to visit the store and see all the things we had on sale or to ask me questions about their antiques.
In fact, sometimes I felt like we were doing too well. When I opened Calvin's Collectibles, it seemed like the store was huge. But eventually it started to feel too small. I thought about all the people who had a connection to the store. I loved the Calvin's Collectibles community.

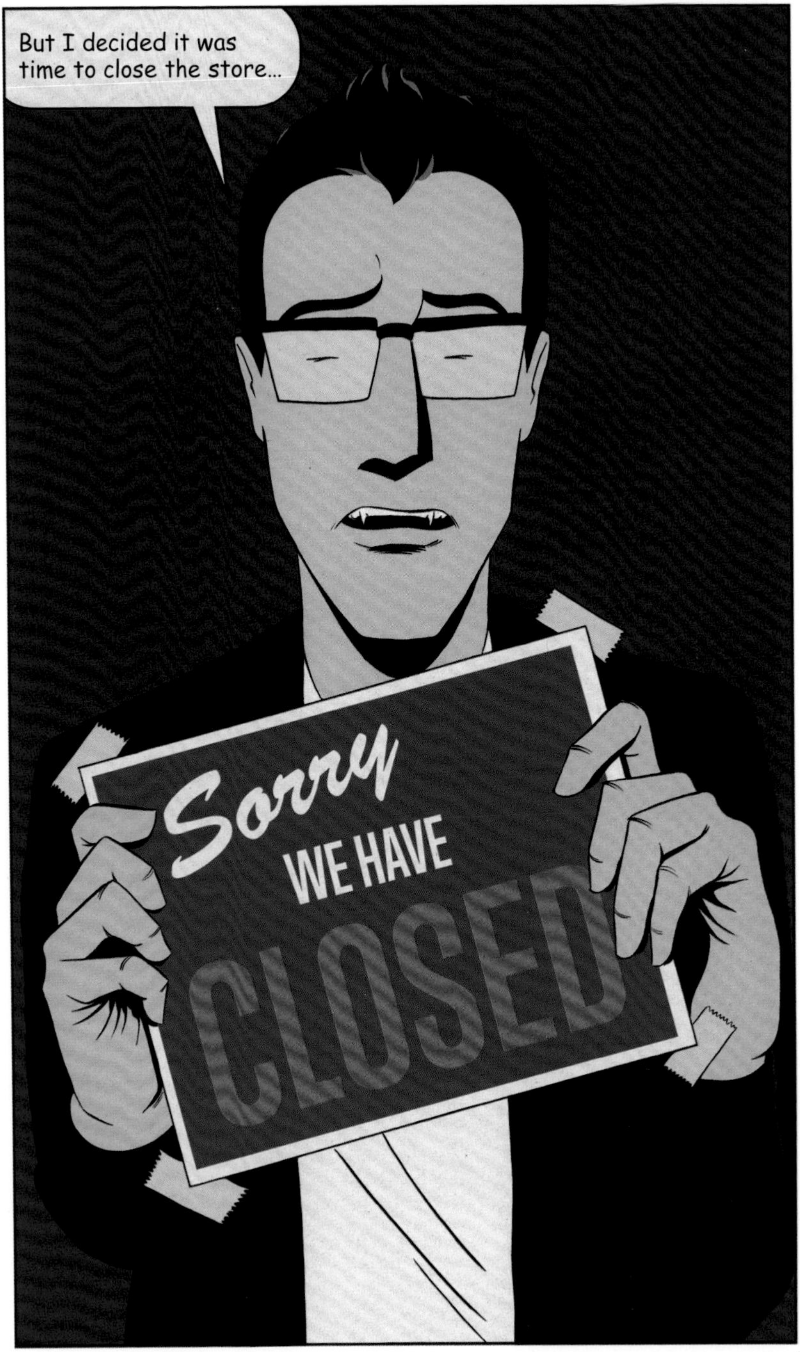
But I decided it was time to close the store...
Sorry WE HAVE CLOSED

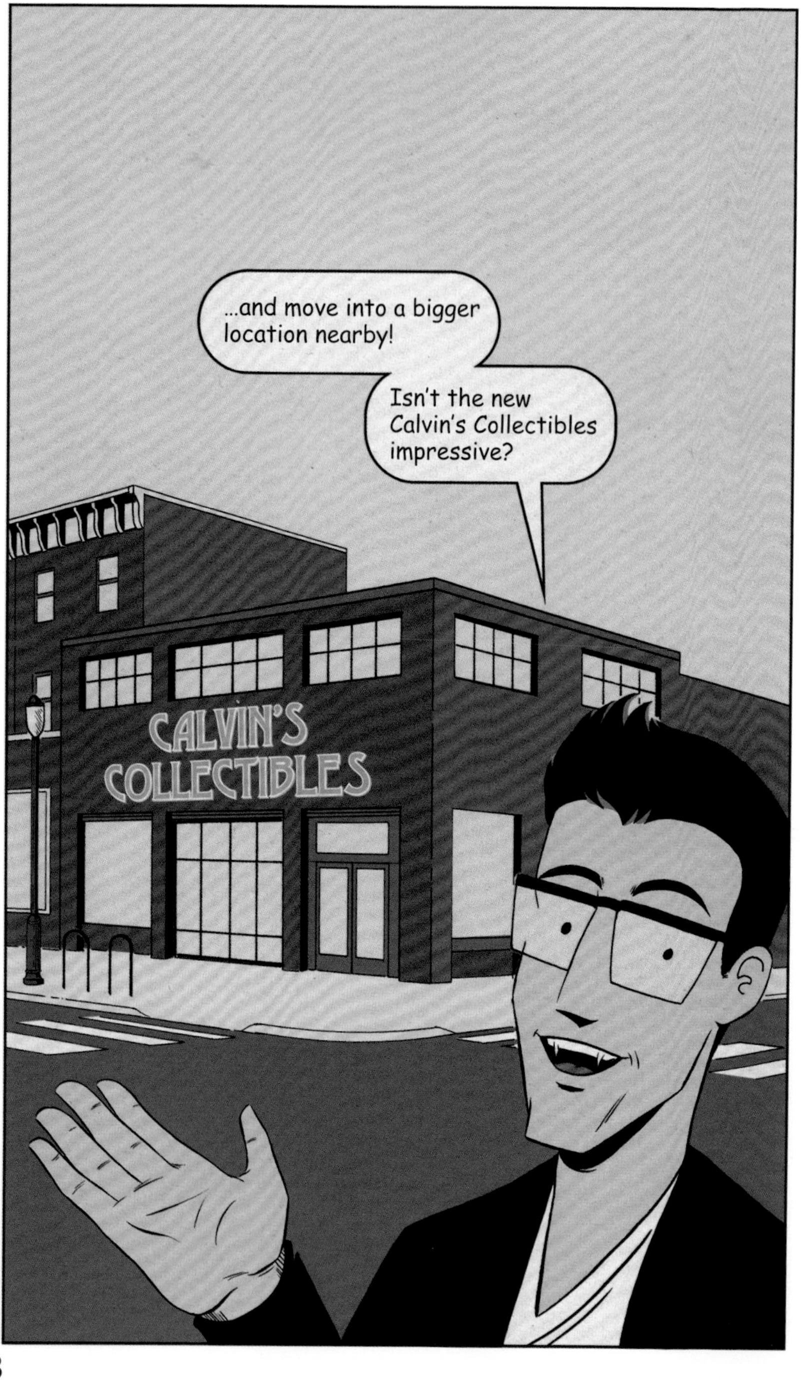
...and move into a bigger location nearby!
Isn't the new Calvin's Collectibles impressive?
CALVIN'S COLLECTIBLES

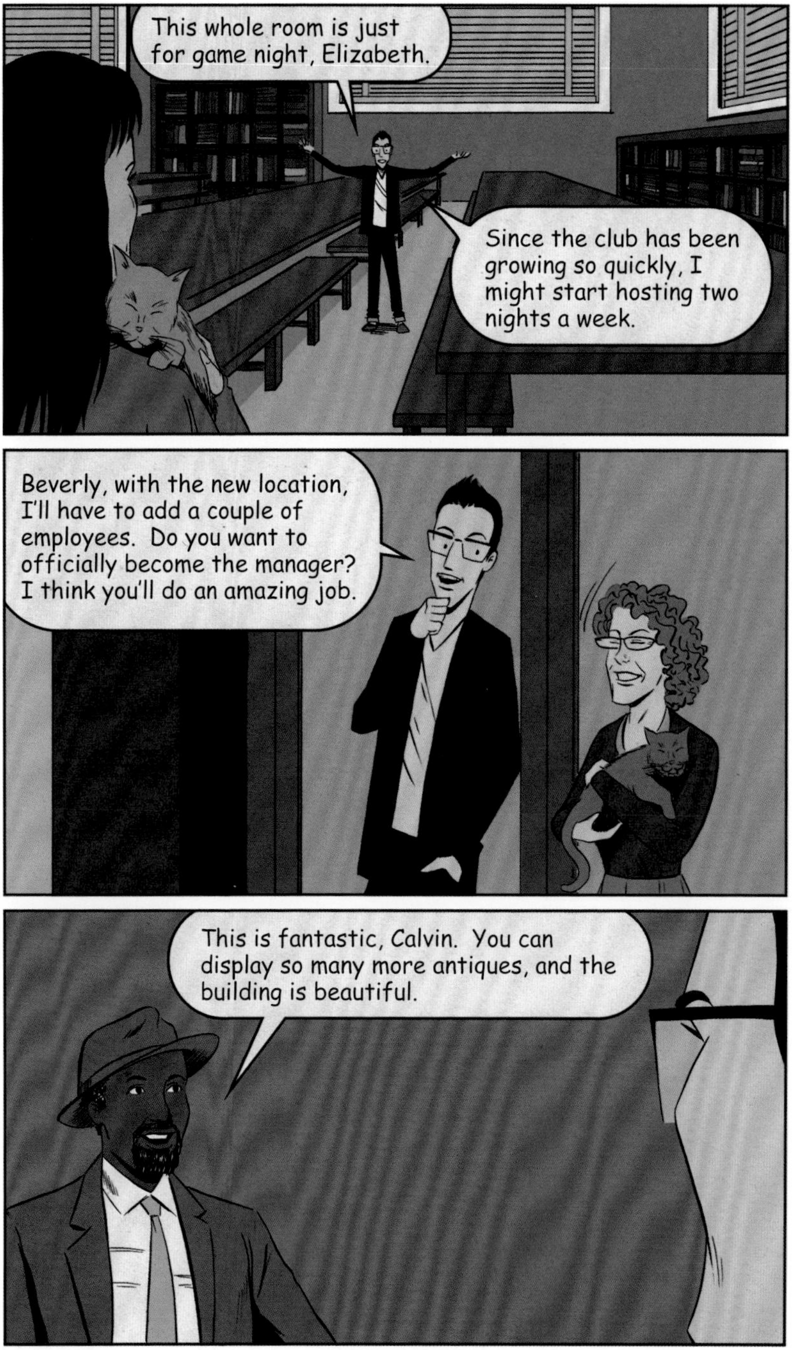
This whole room is just for game night, Elizabeth.
Since the club has been growing so quickly, I might start hosting two nights a week.
Beverly, with the new location, I'll have to add a couple of employees. Do you want to officially become the manager? I think you'll do an amazing job.
This is fantastic, Calvin. You can display so many more antiques, and the building is beautiful.

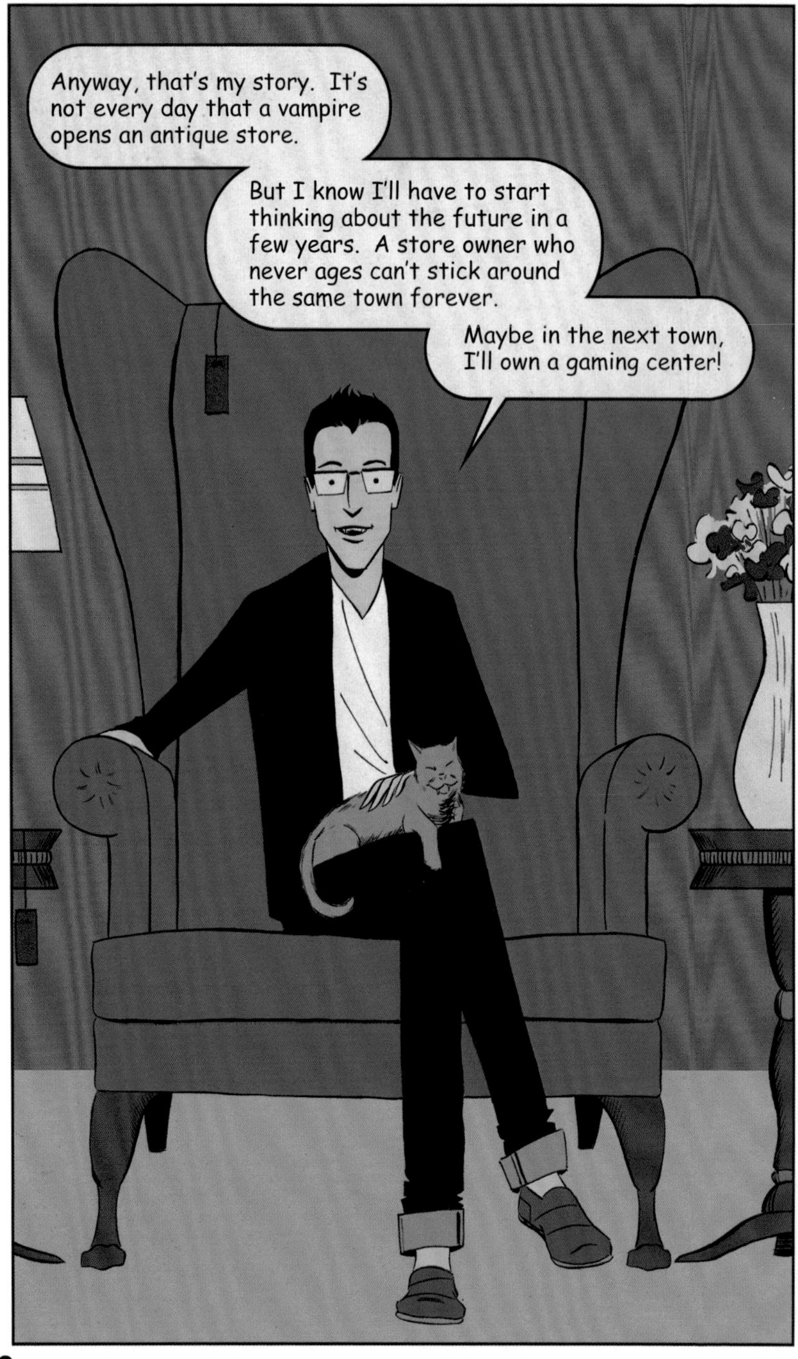
Anyway, that's my story. It's not every day that a vampire opens an antique store.
But I know I'll have to start thinking about the future in a few years. A store owner who never ages can't stick around the same town forever.
Maybe in the next town, I'll own a gaming center!

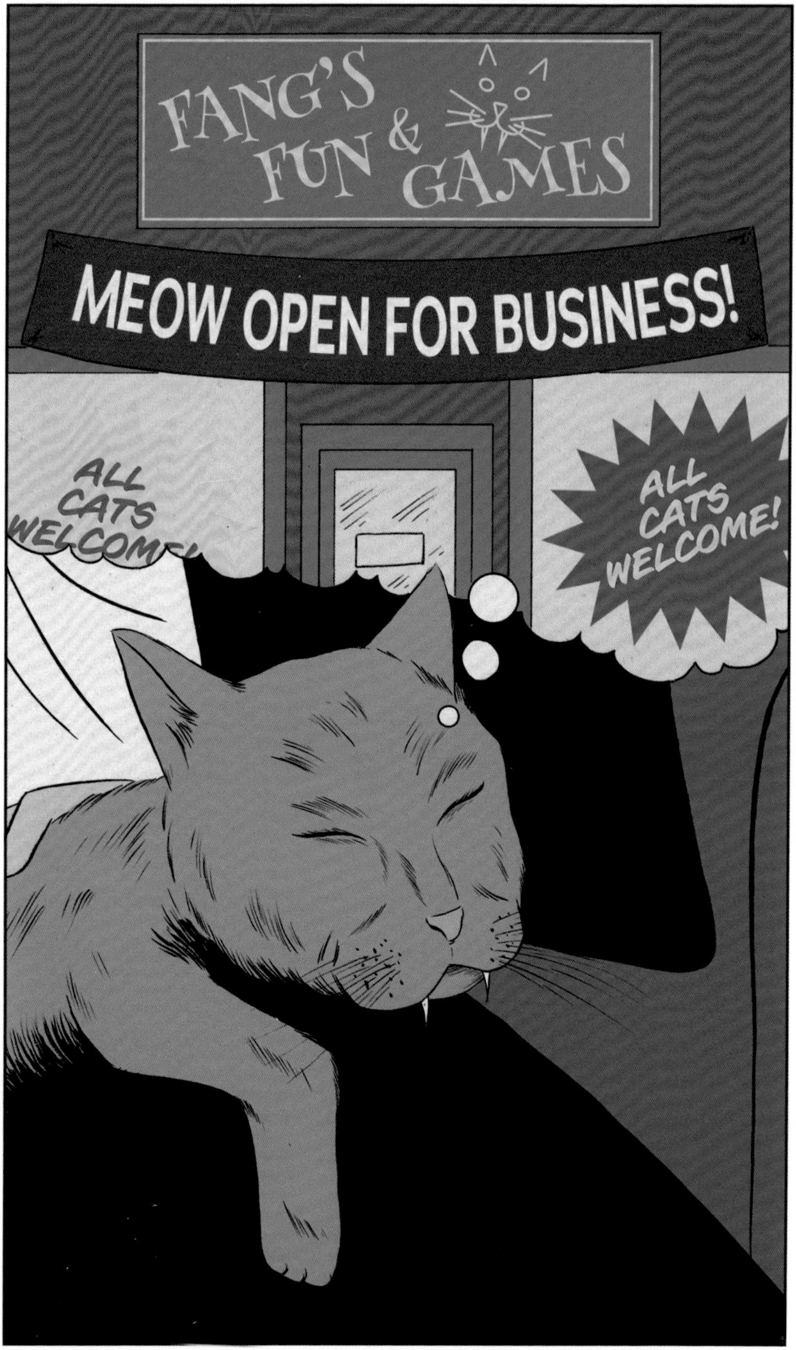
FANG'S FUN & GAMES
MEOW OPEN FOR BUSINESS!
ALL CATS WELCOME!

About Us

The Author
Ben Nussbaum has written many books for children and edited many books for adults. He enjoys shopping for antiques and once worked at an antique store in Indiana. He lives near Washington, DC, with his wife and two kids and a beautiful white cat that is not a vampire and is not named Fang.

The Illustrator
Joseph McDermott remembers drawing the panels from his comic books and creating scenes featuring his favorite cartoon characters when he was a boy growing up in New Jersey. Now based in Philadelphia, he's doing the same thing as a career. Joseph has trained in drawing, painting, sculpture, screen-printing, typography, and photography. He has a Scottish terrier named Monty and a large collection of vinyl albums, and he still loves his comics.